ZOOM BOOM
The Scarecrow *and* Friends

By Joel Brown

Illustrated by
Garrett Myers

Rapier Kids
A Division of Rapier Publishing Company

Zoom Boom The Scarecrow *and* Friends
Copyright © 2015

By Joel Brown
Illustrated by Garrett Myers

ISBN 978-09966083-1-2
Library of Congress Control Number 2015948033

Published by
Rapier Publishing Company
260 W. Main Street, Suite #1
Dothan, Alabama 36301

www.rapierpublishing.com
Facebook: www.rapierpublishing@gmail.com
Twitter: rapierpublishing@rapierpub

Book Cover Design: Garrett Myers/ Book Layout: Rapture Graphics

Follow all the Current Zoom-Boom Book Series by Joel Brown:

Zoom-Boom the Scarecrow and Friends
Be Tidy, or Not?
Be Careful

Thank you for buying this book. It is important to me that my stories are humorous and educational for the adults and children that read them. I was God-inspired to write the Zoom-Boom series of books for my granddaughters. I wanted the stories to be read mainly at bedtime, so that the time shared during those moments would invite questions from the children and discussions about the stories with the parents. I wanted children to have happy thoughts and dreams at bedtime and what better way to do that than to have the comfort and love of a parent reading a *"Zoom-Boom"* bedtime story. With such busy schedules, we often miss opportunities to make our children feel safe and secure while they are awake. So, a soothing voice, a bedtime story, a hug and a kiss before going to sleep is a wonderful way to end the day. This way, the children can feel that *Zoom-Boom* can handle any "Green Eyed Monster" that might be hiding under the bed or in the closet, should they awaken during the night after a nightmare. I hope that you and your children will enjoy reading these stories, as much as I enjoyed writing them.

Author
Joel Brown

On a magical farm are many things to see,
a house, a barn, a field of crops, and many farm animals.

Within this field of crops, there lives a scarecrow named "Zoom-Boom." He is a happy scarecrow. He spends most of his time helping others stay out of trouble.

Farmer Don and his wife Mattie own the farm. They are glad that Zoom-Boom takes care of everyone.

It is a tough job for Zoom-Boom, but he doesn't mind.
He loves being a hero. He wants everyone to be safe at all times.

The animals on this magical farm are like children

to Farmer Don and Mattie. They all have different

personalities and they always listen to Zoom-Boom,

especially when they get in trouble.

Zoom-Boom always tells them the right thing to do!

This makes Farmer Don and Mattie very proud of

Zoom-Boom.

Early every morning, and all throughout the day, you will hear
"Oh, dear," then Zoom, then Boom, as
Zoom-Boom goes to the rescue of someone in trouble.

His name is Zoom-Boom because when he runs,
his legs are moving so fast that he breaks the sound barrier!
Somehow, he knows when there is trouble near, and he always
shows up in the blink of an eye to help.

Zoom-Boom doesn't have to rescue his farm friends too often,

but he is kept quite busy by those pesky crows!

They are his friends too, but they are always getting

into trouble!

After all, Zoom-Boom is a scarecrow, and

he is scared that his "crow" friends are getting into trouble and

that they might hurt themselves or others on the farm.

Zoom Boom's farm friends are...

Graham Quakers, he's a Duck,

Hooks the fish has good luck.

Dirty Bird is quite a Rooster,

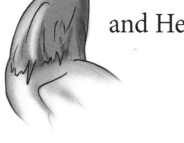

and Hendra Hen is his biggest booster!

Dexter Dogwood is a Dog,

and Hocks the pig is a Hog!

Molly Moo-Cow loves to "moo"

... and Beets the Beetle loves to chew!

Choe-Choe the Kitten is very small,

and Anthony Ant loves to "save" it all.

Skylar Scholar, the Owl of knowledge,

and Beedie the Butterfly loves the foliage!

Harmon the Bird loves to sing...

and Buttons the Bullfrog likes "frilly" things!

Breedie the Horse is full of pride,

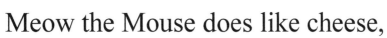

and Leslie the Lamb feels soft outside!

Meow the Mouse does like cheese,

and Rags the Goat says, "Recycle," please!

And then there's Zoom-Boom's pesky crow friends.
Of course, there's Bagpipe: Noisy,

Nelson: Nosey,

Chatman: Chatters,

Carrie: Careless,

Lucy: Loses,

Lyman: Liar,

As you can see, there are lots of friends to keep Zoom-Boom busy!

It's ZOOM to the rescue of someone polluting the lake,

or bullying Choe-Choe, or setting fires!

Or it's

ZOOM to help Carrie cross the street and helping Lucy find her things.

Trouble, Trouble, Trouble!

Zoom-Boom also learns lots of things from his farm friends,

like how Hocks stays in such great physical shape.

Or, how to save his money and other things, like

Anthony Ant always does. You should always "save" for

a rainy day and watch your money tree grow and grow!

Rags the Goat is the recycle king of everything.

"Rags" recycles aluminum cans, clothes

and old newspapers and you can, too!

Zoom-Boom has learned so much about recycling from him.

Ask your teacher or parents how you can help save the

earth, too.

And please stay out of trouble, whatever you do!

You don't want to be a pesky crow that

doesn't know which way to go!

Trouble is so easy to get into, but hard to get out of!

Always be kind to everyone, and learn to be silly and have some fun!

Find the "good" in those you meet,

"HALO"

and all of your rewards will be pleasant and sweet!!!

"X"s "X"s "X"s
"O"s "O"s "O"s
(Kisses & Hugs)

Zoom-Boom is here to help his friends stay out of trouble

and that includes you too!

So, be a friend to everyone you know,

even those pesky crows, and the world will be a better place

to live in!

So boys and girls around the world, get ready when you hear this sound...

ZOOM, BOOM! You know that someone is really safe right now,

because Zoom-Boom the scarecrow has been around!

THE END

About the Author Joel Brown

Joel resides in Decatur, Georgia and is an Atlanta native. He has two precious granddaughters. He loves to read bedtime stories to them. It was in these stories "Zoom-Boom" became alive. He uses his Christian beliefs to tell and share the many adventures of Zoom-Boom and his friends.

About the Illustrator Garrett Myers

Garrett resides in Albany, Georgia. He has been drawing since he was a little boy. He is gifted and talented and uses his gifts and talents to glorify God in all that he draws. He always reminds others that his drawings are creations from God, and his tools are His handiworks.

CPSIA information can be obtained
at www.ICGtesting.com
Printed in the USA
LVOW05s2113230616

493894LV00011B/108/P